Harrison Waits

written and illustrated by
Missy Hagen

ISBN: 978-0-9889048-8-0

Printed in USA 2020

Published by Cresting Wave Publishing, LLC
www.gocwpub.com
"You buy a book. We plant a tree."

Cover background by Vecteezy
Cover and Layout Consultant Lazar Kackarovski

Executive Book Consultant John Chinn

Harrison wakes.

He wees.

He washes
his hands.
Well.

He has waffles, with whipped-cream, honey & huckleberries.

He
waits.

He waits
HOURS and HOURS!

And
HOURS!!

Waiting
by a
huge
window.

While waiting, Harrison hangs out in a wheelbarrow heaped with hay.

While he waits he helps…

Watering
hydrangeas
with a
watering can.

Harrison hammers wood.

Harrison hauls with his handy wagon.

Harrison
is
hungry.

He has a hearty
hamburger heaped
with hot-sauce.

And a wet, wide
wedge of
watermelon.

He waits in a
hammock
with Harry's
wand in hand.

While he waits,
Harrison hurls
horseshoes.

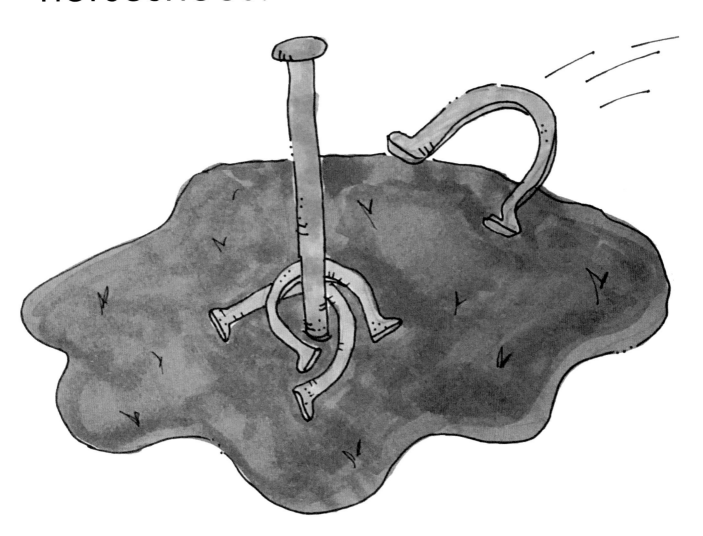

He
hula-
hoops
with his
hips.

He's hiding!

Harrison happily
hops his
hopscotch.

Harrison
hums
on a
harmonica.

He hoops. He scores.

He wears a wide Hero Hat. It helps hours whoosh by!

Wait!

What do I HEAR?

Harrison wiggles
wildly!

HONKING!!

WHEELS!!!

It's Gamma,
Woo-Hoo!

Warm hugs.

How
wonderful!

Worth the WAIT.

Missy Hagen came to children's book writing and illustrating after an eclectic career in fields that seemed to predict such destiny. She has a BA in Elementary Education from Cornell College, spent some years in corporate technical writing, built a popular aerobic dance program in the eighties, raised three children all before returning to college for web and graphic design. She combined her teaching, technical, and design skills as Educational Technology Director for Rochester Community and Technical College for over 10 years. When her grandson, Harrison, was born it sparked the idea for "Harrison Waits" based on his FOUR initials. A story focusing on the letters H and W and about how the rewards of being patient and keeping busy yield an outcome worth waiting for! Missy's watercolor and ink artwork has often been exhibited and featured throughout southeast Minnesota where she resides with her husband.

Made in the USA
Monee, IL
15 November 2020